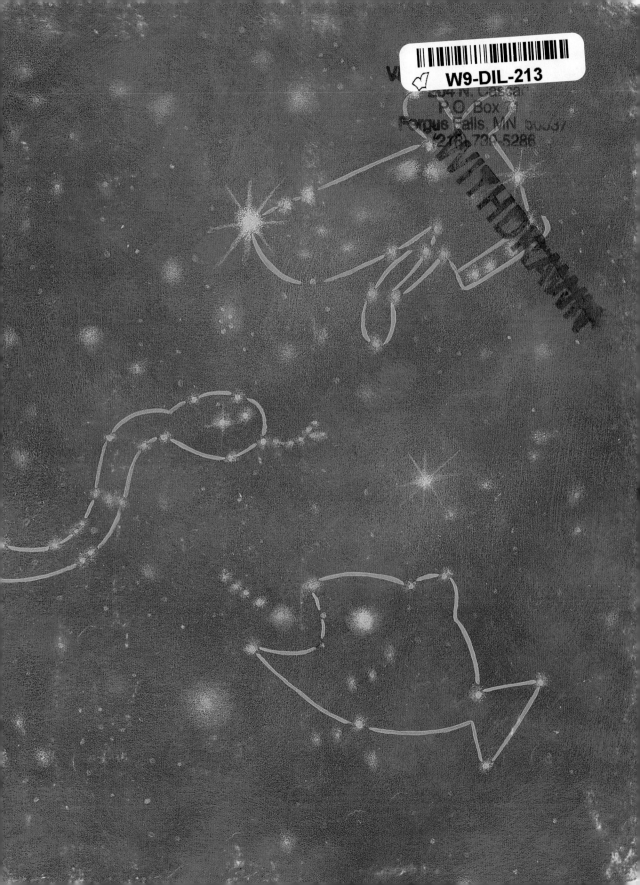

For Paw Paw, wherever you are.

Book design by Susan Van Horn.
Typeset in Fink Heavy.
The illustrations in this book were rendered in
acrylic paints and colored pencils.
Printed in Hong Kong.
ISBN 0-8118-2672-4

Library of Congress Cataloging-in-Publication Data
Graves, Keith.
Pet boy / by Keith Graves.
p. cm.
Summary: After having been kidnapped and taken into space to
become a pet for an alien creature, Stanley finally learns to be
responsible for his many pets at home.
ISBN 0-8118-2672-4
[1. Pets–Fiction. 2. Responsibility–Fiction. 3. Stories in rhyme.]
I. Title.
PZ8.3.G74243 Pe 2000
[E]--dc21
99-050824

Distributed in Canada by Raincoast Books
9050 Shaughnessy Street, Vancouver, British Columbia V6P 6E5

10 9 8 7 6 5 4 3 2 1

Chronicle Books LLC
85 Second Street, San Francisco, California 94105

www.chroniclebooks.com/Kids

Pet Boy

by Keith Graves

chronicle books · san francisco

Stanley collected pets.

He purchased them in singles
and matching colored sets.
Big or small, dry or wet,
he loved to buy new pets.

He studied each one carefully
and played with it awhile,
then he locked it in a cage
and stacked it in a pile.

On Tuesday Stanley's favorite pet
was his giant albacore.
By Wednesday all the "new" was gone.
Stanley soon grew bored.

"Come play with us!" his lonely pets
chirped and barked and purred.
"Feed us! Pet us! Take us out!"
Stanley didn't hear a word.

He wanted something unique
that could swim and fly and hop.
So he looked around and finally found
an undiscovered shop.

Everywhere Stanley looked
the weirdest creatures met his gaze.
Snakes with wings and seven eyes
and singing manta rays.

Wow!

"What do we have here?"
asked a man with turquoise ears.
"I'm sorry if I startled you.
Please put aside your fears.

"I–I'd like to buy a pet," said Stanley,
"one with many skills.
My old pets bore me with their tricks.
I'm looking for some thrills."

uh oh

"I like a thrill as well," said the man,
glancing from shelf to shelf.
"I trade in quirky oddities...
rather like yourself."

A blazing yellow laser zapped Stanley between the eyes.

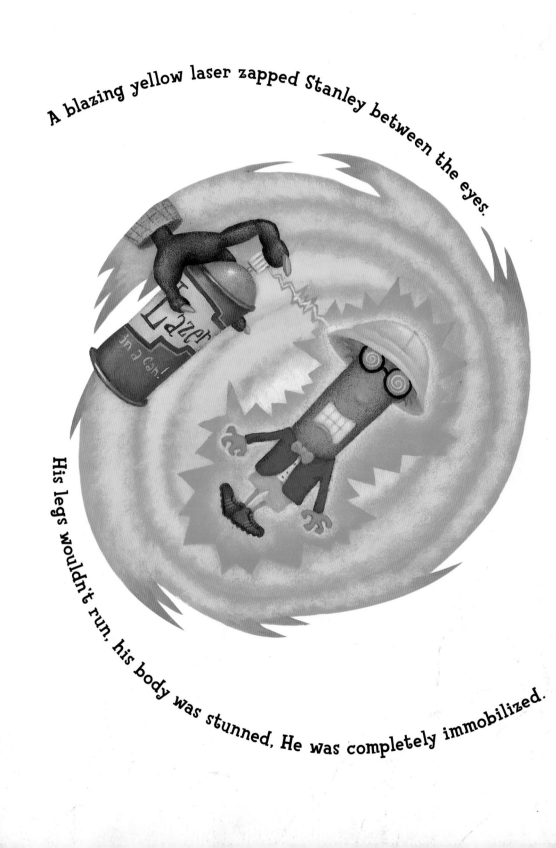

His legs wouldn't run, his body was stunned. He was completely immobilized.

ha ha ha...

Far Out Pets
We deliver!

The man threw Stanley in a cage on his galactic rocket ship.

They blasted off with a sonic boom and into space they zipped.

Over spiral nebulae,
through cold uncharted wastes.
With a bump they finally landed
in a most outlandish place.

Stanley rubbed his eyes.
Things were a blur.
He felt around: a metal cage,
stinky birds with fur.

The room was filled with squawking,
gawking, squealing things galore.
All for sale, including him.
An alien pet store!

Freaky customers shook his cage
when Stanley tried to hide.
A three-eyed buyer said, "I'll take this one!"
Stanley was horrified.

"My name is Jopnar," he drooled and grinned.
"I'll call you Zoo-Zoo-Zar!
And just to keep you safe and sound,
I'll put you in this jar."

Stanley banged and kicked the jar.
He yelled, "Hey, let me go!"
My name is Stanley! I'm not your pet!
I'm just a kid, you know!"

Jopnar said, "Now do some tricks.
Fetch the orb! Bring it here!
Catch the flying saucer as I fling it
through the atmosphere!"

"I'll never do those stupid tricks,
no matter what you say!"
Everything that Jopnar asked,
Stanley disobeyed.

Jopnar wondered, "What have I done
to make my pet so mad?
I'll give him lots of tasty food
and a comfy sleeping pad."

"This food is yucky!" Stanley said.
"I'm not a parakeet.
I think I'll run away from here
when Jopnar falls asleep."

Stanley opened the jar and tiptoed out
and scampered off with glee.
"I don't know where I'll go," he thought,
"but at least I'm finally free."

Stanley watched the stars and longed for home.
He shivered in the frost.

Then something swooped and snatched him up.

A giant iron moth.

The moth brought Stanley to the pound
and dropped him in the clink,
where strays not claimed by end of day
are soon to be extinct.

As the sun began to sink,
Stanley's hopes were running out.
The inmates wailed. Their final meal
was rocks with sauerkraut.

"I need a friend," said Stanley.
"I really miss my pets.
I wonder if they're missing me,
or if they will forget."

The door burst open. Jophar yelled,
"Hey Zoo-Zoo-Zar, it's me!

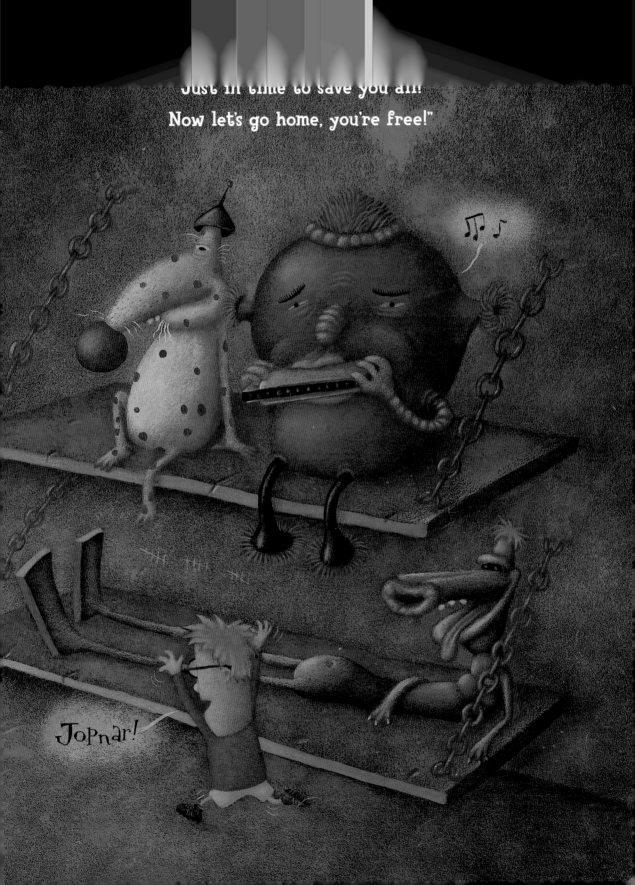

"Thanks," said Stanley. "You saved my life.
Friends like you are few.
But I'm not happy in this jar,
or living here with you.

"My home is in a galaxy
we call the Milky Way.
I must get back. My pets have not
been fed since Saturday.

Jopnar said, "I should return you
to your native habitat!"
So they rented out a space ship
at the local astromat.

They took a shortcut to the Earth,
a twenty-minute flight.
Stanley yelled, "Hooray! I'm home!"
His house was now in sight.

"Go free," said Jopnar,
"I have returned you to the wild.
I must return to the astromat.
They charge me by the mile."

Stanley waved good-bye and ran to see
his long-neglected friends.
"They must be starving, worried sick,
wondering where I've been."

Stanley opened every cage
and said, "I'll offer you a deal.
You're free to go, but if you stay,
you'll never miss a meal."

He treated them like royalty.
He made them lemonade.
He thanked his lucky stars
for all the friends he'd made.

And Stanley's pets
all stayed.

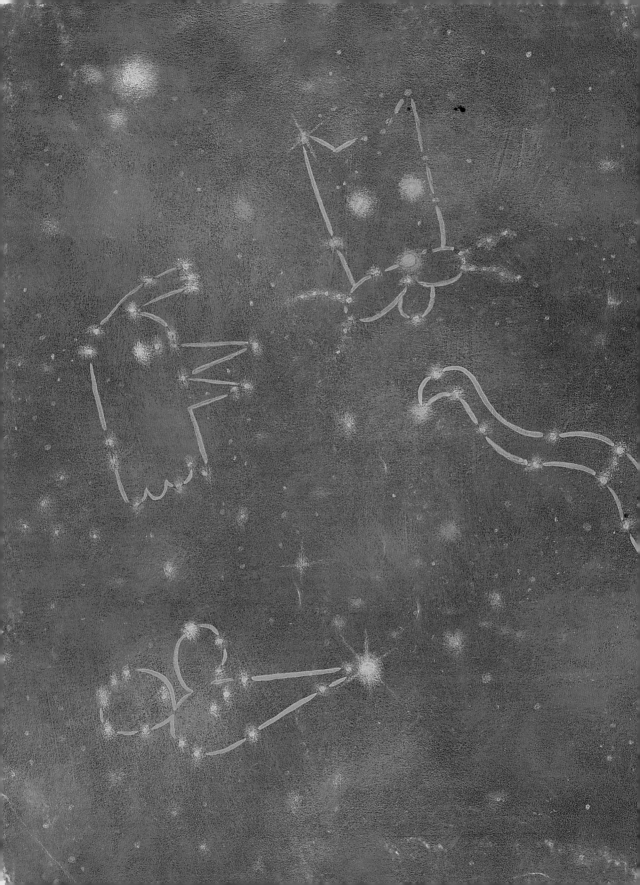